The WOLF'S FOOTPRINT

D0924695

The WOLF'S FOOTPRINT

Susan Price

**Hodder
Children's
Books**

A division of Hodder Headline Limited

A catalogue record for this book is available
from the British Library

ISBN 0 340 85589 4

Typeset by Avon Dataset Ltd, Bidford-on-Avon, Warks

Printed and bound in Great Britain by
Clays Ltd, St Ives plc

The paper and board used in this paperback by
Hodder Children's Books are natural recyclable products
made from wood grown in sustainable forests.
The manufacturing processes conform to the environmental
regulations of the country of origin.

Hodder Children's Books
a division of Hodder Headline Limited
338 Euston Road
London NW1 3BH

Contents

1

NETTLE SOUP

"Gather nettles," said their mother. "Gather all you can."

"But they hurt," Daw said. "They sting."

"Are you hungry? Do you want something to eat? Never mind about the stings, then. We can make nettles into soup."

So they searched for nettles and, when
they found a clump, picked them by the
handful and the armful, piling them
into a basket their mother carried. The
leaves stung fiercely, raising white, hot
lumps on their hands that itched hotly
for hours.

"I wish there were more," their mother said. The nettles were dying as the weather turned colder, and many had already been picked by other people. They carried the nettles home, and their mother stewed them in water. It made a thick, green soup.

"It'll sting our mouths when we eat it!" Daw said.

His sister, Elka, said, "No it won't! Shut up."

"Nettles don't sting when they've been cooked," explained their mother. She served Daw and Elka, and their father and herself a bowl of nettle soup. It tasted horrible and didn't stop them feeling hungry for long.

"Find acorns," said their mother. "I can grind them into flour, and make porridge or bread."

So they hunted all day through the woods, searching for acorns. There were few to be found. It had been a bad year for growing anything. When rain was needed, it had been dry and hot. When warmth was needed, it had been cold and wet. The corn had not grown well – but neither had the wild fruits. Neither had the acorns.

Every man, woman and child in every village nearby was hunting through the woods for acorns, and gathering all they could find. The pigs were rooting for them too. It was tiring, to hunt and hunt, and find so little. Hunger made them cold as well. Their bellies ached and their heads ached. It hurts to be hungry.

But they brought home a basket of acorns, and their mother cracked them, and ground the nuts between stones, to make acorn flour. Then she mixed it with water and made acorn porridge, and they ate a bowl each of that. It was nasty stuff. Nobody ate acorns because they liked them.

But when the acorn flour was all gone, what would they eat then?

"My Granny told me how they ate beech leaves, when they had nothing else," said their father. "We can do that. We can eat beech leaves."

"Winter's coming," said their mother. "The leaves are all withering and blowing away."

They were lying in the bed, huddled under blankets to keep warm. Elka and Daw had their bed in the other corner, on the floor. A mattress stuffed with straw was under them, and blankets over them. Daw was asleep and dribbling, his head on Elka's shoulder. He was exhausted from walking so far, looking for food.

Elka lay awake. She wanted to sleep, but her feet were cold, and her belly ground emptily on nothing. So she lay with her eyes closed, listening to the quiet voices of her mother and father, whispering through the dark from the bed. They thought she was asleep.

"We can eat beech leaves for now," said their father.

"And after that?" their mother asked.

They were both silent for a long time.

"We will starve," said their mother. "You need to eat plenty, just to keep warm, in winter. We have nothing. We shall all shrivel with cold. We shall die."

"Now, now," said their father.

" 'Now, now!' " their mother cried, and Elka heard her sit up. " 'Now, now!?' "

"Ssh. Shh. You'll wake the children."

Elka kept her eyes closed, and pretended to be asleep.

"I wish they would never wake," whispered their mother. "They're happy, asleep. I don't want them to wake, and go hungry day after day, and cry, and cry, when there's nothing I can give them. I don't want to watch them die."

"They won't die!" said their father.

"What's to save them? What is there to eat? Will a roast pig come walking down the street, with a knife stuck in its back, crying, 'Eat me, eat me!'?"

"I can catch a deer," said their father. "Or a rabbit."

"All forest game belongs to the King. He'll have you hanged."

"He won't know about it," their father whispered. "Are you going to tell him? We'll eat the deer, and then the deer won't tell him."

"People will know. Word always gets out. And someone will tell. Someone always does – they'll tell on you for the reward. And then you'll be hanged. What shall I do then? Leave the deer and the rabbits alone."

Their father said nothing.

"We must face it," said their mother. "We have no money. There is no food. Winter is coming. Hope won't feed us."

Still their father said nothing.

"They're already so thin," said their mother. "They won't live until spring."

Elka, her eyes shut, waited for her

father to say something. He said nothing.

"I want you to take them into the forest," said their mother, "and leave them there."

Their father said nothing.

"Take them far in, so they won't find their way back."

"How will that help?" asked their father.

"They'll die quickly! We won't have to watch them starve."

"There are wolves in the forest," said their father.

"Being eaten by wolves would be quicker than starving, and less painful in the end. It would only take a moment. And anyway, there are roads through the forest. If they find their way to one, maybe some rich traveller from far away will take them home with him, and feed them."

"You're mad," their father said. "I might catch a rabbit tomorrow. You'll feel better then."

"A rabbit won't feed us all! Do you want to watch your children die slowly? Take them into the wood and leave them."

"I'm going to sleep," their father said, and Elka heard nothing more whispered between her parents after that. She didn't sleep herself, but lay awake, hungry and cold, for hour after dark hour, until slow, grey morning came.

They had cold water for breakfast.

2

Into the Woods

"Come on, you two," their father said. "Let's go into the woods and see what we can find."

Elka and Daw sat side by side on the bench outside the hut, and looked at him. There was a cold wind blowing, and it threw a spattering of rain into their faces. Daw was fretful and hungry, and didn't want to walk.

Their father held out his hands to them. "Come on. There might be nuts! There might be blackberries. Mushrooms, maybe."

At the thought of food, Daw slipped

from the bench and went to his father. He was too little to know that all the mushrooms had been picked and all the blackberries eaten. He looked over his shoulder at his sister. "Come on, Elka."

Elka sat where she was, remembering how, in the night, her mother had told their father to take them into the forest and leave them. He hadn't agreed – but perhaps he meant to do it anyway.

"Elka doesn't want any blackberries," said their father. "Come on then – we'll eat them all ourselves!" And, hand in hand, Daw and his father walked towards the trees.

Elka watched them go for a while, then got up and walked after them. She couldn't bear to think of little Daw by himself in the woods.

They walked slowly and rested often, because all of them were hungry and tired. But every time they rested, their father would soon say, "Up you get; on we go." Slowly, walking and resting, walking and resting, they went a long way.

The paths in the wood became more overgrown as they went further from the village, more tangled and twisting. Elka tried to remember which way the village was, but soon she couldn't tell. They found a few blackberries, but not many, though their father always said, "There'll be more further on – where other people haven't been."

And they did find a bush, with a few blackberries still on it. They found it as the light was deepening and turning golden, so Elka knew it was late in the afternoon. Daw was picking and eating berries as fast as he could, thinking of nothing else, his hands and face stained purple. Elka picked them and ate too, and they laughed at each other's purple lips and tongues.

"You stay and eat as many as you can," said their father. "I'll go on a bit, and see if there are some more . . ." And he moved away into the trees.

"Don't leave us!" Elka said suddenly.

He stopped and looked back. "I'm not going to leave you," he said, and laughed. And he vanished into the leaves and dappled light.

Daw took no notice, but busily picked more berries. Elka stared at the place where their father had disappeared, thinking that soon it would be dark. She heard a branch swish as her father moved it, and a bird that he had scared fly up, but then she heard nothing more. A silence settled over the woods.

"We should run after him," she thought, and grabbed Daw's hand. But Daw didn't want to go with her. "There are berries left," he said.

"We've got to go home now. We've got to find father," Elka said.

Daw leaned back, pulling against her hand. "Father's going to come back for us."

"Come *on!*" Elka dragged him along.

She hurried into the bushes where her father had gone, dragging Daw behind her. She was looking for her father's tall body, for his back. Everywhere she looked, she saw nothing but branches and red leaves and grass. Their father had left them.

Standing still, Elka listened. Her heart was beating fast, and she was breathing hard, but she tried to listen through those sounds. A bird called away to her left – that was where her father was! He had disturbed the bird.

She dragged Daw that way. They pushed through overhanging branches and ducked beneath boughs, they scrambled up a soft, grassy bank, and splashed through a cold, muddy stream. They saw and heard nothing of their father. And now they were more lost than before. It was darker. Everything about the wood was fading into darkness. Elka knew that she couldn't even find her way back to the place where their father had left them.

Daw cried, because he was tired, and he wanted to go back and eat more berries. "Daddy won't know where to find us!" he said.

Elka stopped and sat down, because she was tired too. They had been hungry for so long that they tired quickly. She pulled Daw into her lap. "We'll stay here," she said. "He'll find us. If he wants to, he'll find us."

Daw grizzled in her lap. "I want the berries. You made me come away from the berries. And now it's dark."

"Never mind," Elka said.

"I'm cold," Daw said. "When is Daddy coming back?"

"Soon," Elka said. "Soon."

But even when it was so dark that they could only see each other's faces as pale smudges, even then their father hadn't come back. "Why doesn't Daddy come?" Daw asked.

Elka wondered whether to tell him what she knew. But then he would cry and that would make things worse. So she kept quiet.

"A bear might come," Daw said. "And eat us."

Elka hugged him, but said nothing, remembering what her mother had whispered about a quick death in the forest being better than slowly starving. Maybe that was so, but she was afraid of bears.

"A ghost might come," Daw said, in a little wail.

"There are no such things as ghosts," Elka said, but her own voice wavered, because she didn't believe it. Which would be worse? A ghost or a bear? She couldn't tell.

In the darkness, a shadow moved, and

something green glinted in a patch of moonlight.

Another shadow drifted among the trees, grey in the darkness, and there was another glint.

Green eyes looked at her from the darkness.

She looked another way, and there were more green eyes.

Green eyes and grey shadows, all about them in the darkness, watching.

3

The Paw Print

"Look at the dogs," Daw said. "Will they bite us?"

Elka wanted to tell him that the dogs wouldn't hurt them, but she knew that they weren't tame village dogs. The grey shadows that watched them with green eyes were wild wolves from the forest and the dark. "They are going to eat us," she thought. "Just like mother said. But will it be quick?"

She wanted to run away, but was so afraid that she couldn't move from where she sat. Maybe, if they kept very, very still, the wolves wouldn't notice them. Running would do no good anyway – wolves could run much faster than she could. Fast enough to catch deer. And little Daw couldn't run fast at all. The wolves would catch him with one spring.

Hugging Daw tight, she closed her eyes, and waited for the first wolf bite.

She waited and waited, and made a little sob, and still waited – but nothing touched her. There was no sound, except for the wind in the branches above them. And then she felt something – not a bite, but a faint puff of air. A twitching against her skin, the tickling of a whisker. A cold nose was sniffing at her.

She moaned in fright and opened her eyes wide. As she feared, a big, grey wolf was standing so close that his black nose almost touched her. The strong, musky scent of his thick fur filled her nose. She screwed her eyes shut again.

There was another snuff at her neck, and she opened her eyes to see the wolf sniffing at Daw, who squirmed in her lap. The wolf's big ears twitched, and then he left them, trotting back to the dim grey shapes in the darkness. The shapes moved. They were the other wolves, sitting and lying at a distance. The big wolf went among them, his tail held high, sniffing at one here, and

nudging another with his nose. It was as if he spoke to them, silently.

Three wolves rose and came loping over to the children. Elka hugged Daw tight again, but she wasn't as scared as she'd been before. The three wolves came close and snuffled at their hair and necks, making Daw giggle. One of the wolves licked Elka's face and ear with a big, hot, wet tongue, and Elka wrinkled her nose because its breath smelt so bad.

The wolves turned themselves round and round, like dogs settling to sleep, and lay down close by them. Elka and Daw were encircled with wolves.

The other wolves, led by the biggest, trotted away into the darkness of the wood.

Elka sat very still and stiff, afraid at

having such big, wild animals so near. They hadn't hurt them yet, but maybe they weren't hungry and were saving them to eat later? Daw stroked the nearest wolf, pushing his hand deep into the thick fur at the animal's neck. The wolf reared up its head and looked at him, and then opened its mouth, showing its long teeth, lolled out its tongue and panted, as if laughing.

Elka felt warmer, because the wolves lying around her gave her the heat of their bodies, and kept the wind off her. With the warmth came a feeling of being very, very tired. Her eyes kept closing and her head falling, and she would wake with a jump. Still the wolves did nothing to hurt or threaten them, and she sat a little easier. It was hard work keeping herself stiff and

still, and she couldn't keep it up for long.

One of the wolves snored, and she almost laughed. "If the wolves were going to hurt us," she thought, "they would have hurt us by now." And she was almost too tired to care. So she lay down, and Daw snuggled beside her. In the middle of the three wolves, warm and safe, they slept.

They woke to wolf-song. There was grey morning light, and their guardian wolves had left them to gambol round the big leader wolf, and the returning pack. They howled to greet them. They yipped and yapped with happiness, and licked each other, wagged tails and nipped ears. Elka and Daw sat in the grass, watching the grey shapes in the half-light. They were chilly without the wolves to keep them warm. Hunger was hurting them again, making even their finger-ends ache.

The big leader wolf came over to them and sniffed them, and others came round them, rubbing their fur against them, snuffling, and licking their faces with big, hot, wet tongues. "Hello," Elka said, stroking them. "Hello, then." Their fur was deep and thick and warm.

The leader wolf shuddered, and stretched its neck, and heaved – and spewed from its mouth a pile of steaming meat. It was offering the children food, just as it would offer food to its cubs. The wolf-spew smelt horrible. And yet, at the same time, it smelt meaty and good too, because the children had been hungry for so long. Daw grabbed a handful of the spewed-up meat and ate it.

He grinned at Elka. "It's good!"

When she saw that, Elka grabbed a handful for herself. It was soft, hot and wet. She shoved it into her mouth before she could think any more about it, and it tasted of meat. She ate more, and squabbled with Daw for the next fistful. With every gulp, they felt stronger.

It was deer meat. No one hanged the wolves for catching deer.

The wolves threw themselves on the grass and watched the children eat; and while they watched, the light grew stronger, bringing faint greens, browns and yellows to the leaves around them.

The lead-wolf rose then, and barked. He trotted away, looked over his shoulder, and barked again. The wolves rose, to follow him, and several of them nudged the children, even nipping them lightly when they didn't move. The wolves were leaving, and wanted the children to go with them.

Elka took Daw's hand and pulled him

to his feet, and they followed the narrow grey backs of the wolves as they trotted through the thickets of the forest. Two wolves followed them, nudging them with their noses to hurry. Elka marvelled at how much stronger her legs felt beneath her. She was in a good mood now, too, and felt like singing, because she was still alive. It was all because of the food the wolves had brought them.

"Where's Daddy?" Daw asked, as they followed the wolves. "Where's Mammy?"

"Maybe the wolves will bring us to them," Elka said, but she thought to herself that they were safer with the wolves. Their parents had left them in the forest to die. The wolves had kept them warm and fed them.

The wolves led them down a bank

to the muddy edge of a brown stream. They drank with a lollopy, splashing noise; and the children drank too. The water was cold, and made them shudder, but it was good.

The lead wolf came to Elka and gave her a strong but gentle shove with its nose, so that she fell over into the soft grass and mud. She thought the wolf wanted to play, but, with its nose, it pointed. It nudged her, and pointed again, this time with its paw as well as its nose.

The wolf was showing her a footprint in the mud. A wolf's print. Water had filled the print. The wolf looked at her with brown eyes that gleamed with amber light, and lowered its nose to the print. It licked up a drop of water, and looked at her again.

Did the wolf want her to drink from the paw print?

Elka got down on her hands and knees and pretended to drink. The wolf wagged its tail and gave a little, eager skip.

So Elka put her lips to the water in the paw print, and sucked up a little of the water. It tasted of earth and leaves.

She raised her head and felt so strange. The world was moving about her. The trees were stretching up and becoming taller – or she was shrinking and becoming smaller. All colour was draining away to grey, but her nose tingled with new smells.

Daw gave a loud cry and pointed at her. He didn't look the same as before. Everything about him was grey, and his outline was fuzzier. She only saw him clearly when he moved.

"Elka!" he said, but the rest of what he said was mere noise, like the wind brushing through the leaves and the stream bubbling by.

Then he knelt down and drank from the wolf paw print too.

And, in the blinking of her eye, he turned into a wolf!

4

The Hunt

To be a wolf is a good life.

The wolves never went hungry. They hunted. With quick pounces and bites they caught squirrels or rabbits. They called the pack together with wolf-song and hunted deer.

The hunt was silent. The bravest and

biggest wolf raced ahead and seized the deer by the nose, risking its sharp hooves. Others caught its legs in their strong teeth. The deer was dragged down by the whole weight of the pack, and the whole pack shared the deer's meat, even those who hadn't helped to catch it, like Elka and Daw.

The wolves ate berries, worms and beetles too, though these were tid-bits, a mere change of taste for amusement.

As wolves, Elka and Daw soon grew strong again. Often they sat and looked at each other, admiring their thick fur, which became thicker and more glossy as the year turned colder. They flicked their quick, pointed ears, and waved their tails. It was wonderful to sniff the air and to know, by the smells, that a mouse had run by this way a little time before, and that a fox was hiding over there, in the thicket.

It was wonderful to run with the pack, and feel the strength rippling through their bodies, from shoulder to haunch, to feel the wind passing through their fur. When they had been people, and starving, they hadn't been able to run and jump like that – but it was hard to remember the time when they had been people. They could not think of that time. If they tried, it slid away from their minds and melted away like fog, like a dream. They were wolves, and they thought and remembered as wolves – they thought of the pack, and of hunting; and they remembered smells and sounds.

The wolves knew that the children were glad to be with them. They saw

Elka play with Daw, rolling him over, growling and pretending to bite him – then springing away and pretending to be scared when he chased her. It was plain that they were glad to be wolves, and the wolves understood that, without words.

But the wolf pack hunted too well. They killed so many of the King's deer, that the King's foresters sent messages to court. "The wolves in our forest grow too many and too bold," they said. "We ask your permission to kill them."

The King could have given his permission, and his foresters would have set traps in the woods. But the King thought he would like the excitement of a wolf-hunt. So the King himself came to the forest, with his royal huntsmen, to hunt and kill the wolves that dared to hunt his deer.

The King rode into the forest with a troop of horsemen. Bells jingled on the horses' brightly-coloured harnesses, and gold fringes decked their saddle-cloths. With them came beaters, on foot, and men holding big gaze-hounds in leash, and men who blew horns. They crashed through the growth of the forest, hoofs clumping on the forest rides, shouting, laughing and blowing horns.

The wolves heard them when they were many miles away. Silently, they left their den and jogged away from the noise, seeking quieter places.

But the men, and their noise, were everywhere. Soon the yelling and breaking of branches was in front of them again. When they turned from it, the noise followed them. Now it was to their left, now to their right.

The wolves ran in every direction to escape the hunt, and soon each wolf found itself alone. They twisted and turned through the forest thickets, trying to join each other again, but they would glimpse a horse through the leaves and turn away – they would hear the trumpeting of a horn too close, too close, and turn away again. The hunt split the pack.

Daw was alone. Always his sister, Elka, had been with him; as a boy, as a wolf. He had trotted by Elka's side, he had slept beside her – but now she was gone. The other wolves, too – the big wolves, the strong wolves who had cared for them – all gone. Alone, he ran for his life.

The hounds found his track. He heard them bay he heard their heavy paws scrambling after him. Looking over his shoulder, he saw them, coming fast through the branches and leaves, leaning as they raced – so fast!

He tried to run faster still, but felt the first failing in his muscles. He heard their teeth snap at his tail. His paws felt the thump of horses' hooves through the ground. Horns bellowed and shrilled.

Daw leapt a stream and struggled to climb the bank. A hound was above him, looking down with bared teeth. Behind him was a splash as another hound leapt into the water. He saw their glaring eyes, their red tongues and white teeth, and he threw up his head, crying, "Elka! Elka! Help me!"

The King, riding his horse along by

the stream's side, ducking his head to avoid branches, heard the cry. He asked his huntsmen, "Who called? Who called for help?"

Then he saw the wolf cub desperately splashing in the stream, turning and twisting to avoid the teeth of the hounds. He saw the cub drag itself halfway up the stream's muddy bank, only to slip back as a hound snapped its big teeth at the cub's leg. The King was watching and saw the wolf cub open its mouth and cry, with a human voice, "Help me, Elka! Help me!"

The King beat back the hounds nearest to him, and urged his horse down the bank into the stream. "Beat them off!" he yelled to his men. "Save the cub! Take it alive – catch it! Don't you hear it call for help?"

The huntsmen waded into the stream, beating off the hounds and leashing them. Others caught the little wolf cub, though it snapped at them and struggled. They bound its feet together and brought it to the King, who reached down from his big horse and took the cub in his arms.

"Speak again!" he said to it. "What are you?"

But the cub was exhausted and afraid. It trembled in the King's arms, and showed the whites of its eyes in fear, but it did not speak.

"It spoke," said the King. "It cried out, 'Elka! Help me!' Didn't you hear it?"

The huntsmen struggled to hold the excited hounds, and didn't look at the King. Some of them thought they had heard the wolf cub call out, but hoped they were mistaken. Others had heard nothing but their own shouting.

"If it did call out, King," said the leading huntsman, "then let it go. Or kill it."

"Kill it!" said the King. "Are you mad?"

"It can bring no good luck with it," said the huntsman. "If it called out, then it must be a witch in disguise, or something bad. Kill it."

"No," said the King. "I shall keep it."

Now the huntsmen did look at each other, and they weren't happy. "There's no luck in keeping a thing like that, King."

"I think there may be," said the King. "Not every king has a talking wolf!"

And the King carried Daw the wolf cub back to the royal hunting lodge on his saddlebow.

5

THE HUNTING LODGE

The King thought his hunting lodge was a small place where he lived while he was hunting.

It was bigger and more crowded than any place that Daw had ever seen, as a boy or as a wolf. To Daw it was a vast and frightening palace.

There was a great hall where the King and all his huntsmen and friends ate and slept. There were stables, and kennels, and mews for the falcons, and lodgings for all the men who looked after the dogs and the horses and the birds.

There were workshops, where horses could be shoed, and where leather harnesses could be repaired.

There was a huge kitchen, where food for all these people could be cooked, and bread baked, and animals slaughtered. There were smells and stinks of cooking meat, burning hooves, charring wood, and dung, and horses and people.

There was so much noise. The tramping of feet and the yelling and chatter of voices. The barking of dogs and whinnying of horses. Hammering from the forges; clattering from the kitchens.

Daw's ears were so full of noise, and his nose so bothered with smells, that he didn't know what to do or which way to turn. Should he track the sheep and pigs he could smell, and bite them? Should he follow the scent of burning meat? Should he cower from the din of shouting voices and the row of hammering? Most of all he wanted to run away, but he couldn't do that, because the King had fastened a thick collar about his neck, with a heavy chain.

The King dragged him into a stable, where the light was dim, and there was a strong smell of horses. Daw could hear them shifting in the stalls, whuffling air through their noses and stamping their hooves. They were nervous because they could smell wolf.

Daw hated the stables because the horses reminded him of the hunt. He dug in his paws and fought against his collar, but the King dragged him into an empty stall and fastened the end of his leash to a strong post. There was thick straw on the floor, to make it comfortable.

The King crouched in front of him and held out pieces of meat. He said, "Speak again. Speak!"

Daw was hungry. He darted forward, snatched a piece of meat, but then pressed himself into a corner at the back of the stall. Now that the hounds were no longer snapping at his heels, he couldn't have spoken if he'd wanted to; and he no longer understood the human words. He was merely lonely and frightened.

For a long time the King tried to coax his new pet into talking. "Speak! Say just one word and you can have this other piece of meat." But at last, when the cub only cowered and shivered like any other frightened animal, the King became bored. He went away, shutting the door of the stall behind him. Daw was left alone, still shivering, in the horse-scented, hay-scented gloom of the stables.

The long hours of the night went by slowly. Daw listened to the horses stamp and kick their stalls. They hated him being in their stable. He was lonely without Elka and the other wolves, and hungry too. He went close to the door

of the stall and tried to shout. Only the whimpering and howling of a wolf cub came out – a lonely and frightened wolf cub calling for his pack. The horses whinnied in terror and kicked their stalls with great booms, like the noise of a big drum. Grooms ran into the stable to quieten them, and they kicked the door of Daw's stall and yelled, "Shut that row or we'll wring your neck!"

They wouldn't have dared to harm the King's wolf cub, but Daw didn't know that, or even understand the words. He was only frightened by the noise and threat, and went to the corner at the back of his stall where he curled up small. If he had been in the shape of a boy, he would have cried; but wolves can't cry.

* * *

The next day, the King came again, unfastened his chain from the post and dragged him from the stall. Daw was hauled and dragged across the stable-yard and into the noise and heat of the hall in the hunting lodge. It was crammed full with shouting people, with staring faces, and there was too much noise and too many smells – of food, of wine, of wood burning, of flesh, blood and sweat. Daw tried to run away, but the King stooped and grasped his collar and dragged him the whole length of the hall to the royal table.

There Daw cowered beneath the table, near the King's feet. The dogs growled at him and showed their teeth.

The King sat in his big chair and shouted out the story of how the wolf had been captured. "It cried out in a

human voice! I heard it!" And the King dragged Daw from beneath the table, into the centre of the hall, so that all the red faces and many, many bright eyes could stare at him.

"Shout out again, wolf!" they said, and bones and bits of meat were thrown at him from all sides.

Daw was terrified, and ran about at

the end of his chain, trying to escape. Was the rest of his life to be lived like this, as a captured wolf, struggling at the end of a chain? He could not bear it.

At the end of the feast, the King dragged Daw towards the door. When Daw saw that he was being taken from the hall, he bounded to the end of his chain and trotted willingly ahead. He wanted nothing more than to leave the hall, and its noise, and its stinks. Even the lonely stable, with all the frightened horses, would be better.

"See!" said the King. "He walks on his chain! I shall teach him to be a good wolf!"

It was dark outside the hall, and there were men waiting, with torches, to guide the King to his lodging. Daw was thirsty and no one, through the long, hot evening, had thought to give him a drink. Looking this way and that with quick wolf-eyes, he saw a gleam of water in a patch of mud. He tugged on his chain, tugging towards it: he bunched up his shoulders and used all his strength to pull the King over to the little puddle. Reaching out his tongue, he lapped up a splash of water. It lay in a man's footprint.

In the blink of an eye, Daw turned into a boy, with a collar about his neck, and a chain stretching from it to the King's hand.

6

Daw and The King

The King dropped the chain he held, and stepped back. The men with him pulled swords from their scabbards, ready to protect their king from this witchcraft. They drew back their sharp blades, ready to strike, and Daw would have been chopped down by swords on every side if the King had not shouted:

"No! Don't! Stand back and leave him!"

The men did not want to obey. They were afraid and they wanted to kill the thing that had frightened them. But they lowered their swords.

The King had seen Daw flinch, like any boy faced with angry men. He did not think this boy was dangerous, even if he could turn into a wolf.

The King and Daw looked at each other.

"You were my wolf," said the King.

Daw didn't know what to say. He started to cry and said only, "I am Daw."

"What are you, Daw?" the King asked. "A boy or a wolf?"

Daw cried harder. "I was a wolf with the wolves. I wish I was a wolf

again. I wish I was a wolf."

"A shape-shifter!" said the captain of the King's guard. "Kill it!"

But the King waved his hand to tell the man to be quiet. The King crouched in front of Daw and spoke to him softly. "Were you always a wolf?"

"I was a boy," Daw wept. "Before. With my mother and father. It was better being a wolf. Not so hungry."

The King stood and held out his hand to Daw. "Let's you and me go and sit by the fire," he said. "Yours is a story I should like to hear."

So Daw, hand in hand with the King, and with the collar and chain still round his neck, walked through the hall of the hunting-lodge while everyone – all the King's men and servants – stared to see such a sight. At the door of the King's private rooms, the King stopped, and took the collar from around Daw's neck. He threw it aside, and it landed with a crash on the wooden floor. Daw was glad to be rid of the heavy thing.

The King's private room was small and warm. A large fire burned on the hearth, and beautiful, coloured hangings covered the walls and kept out the draughts. The King himself picked up a small stool and set it beside the fire. "Sit there," he said to Daw.

While Daw enjoyed the heat of the fire, the King poured a cup of weak ale for him, and also handed him a plate of bread and meat. "Eat all you want," the King said, and seated himself in a high-backed chair on the other side of the fire.

"Tell me about your mother and father," the King said.

Daw found it hard to remember them. "They were kind to me," he said. "But they never had enough to eat. And we were always cold because it was hard to find enough wood to burn."

"Why didn't they have enough to eat?" the King asked.

Daw looked at him, surprised that he didn't know. "Nothing grew, sir. It was

too wet and too cold. We ate nettles and acorns, but they don't stop you being hungry. I was always hungry."

"Nettles and acorns?" said the King in disgust. "Why didn't you catch fish or rabbits?"

Daw was astonished. "We aren't allowed to hunt in the forests, sir. They belong to the King. You're hanged, if you hunt in the King's forests, sir."

"Ah," said the King, and was quiet for a while. "Do you want some more to eat? Some more ale?" When Daw's plate and cup were full again, the King said, "Tell me how you came to be a wolf."

"Daddy took us to look for berries in the forest, but we got lost – Elka and me, my sister and me. We got lost and couldn't find Daddy, and it got dark, and we were scared. But the wolves came."

"Weren't you scared of the wolves? I would have been."

"We were scared – but the wolves were good to us. And they showed us how to change into wolves."

"How?" the King asked.

"You drink water from a wolf's footprint."

"Is that all?" said the King. "Is it so easy? But I don't think I'd be brave enough to try it."

"I wish I was back with Elka and the wolves," Daw said.

"But they are animals, sleeping cold and wet in the forest," said the King, "eating their meat raw."

"They were kind to us," Daw said. "They kept us warm, and fed us, and played with us. *You* hunted me."

"I thought you were a wolf, stealing

my deer," said the King.

"You love your deer, don't you?" said Daw. Now he was full of meat and ale, he was falling asleep. "You hunt the wolves who steal them. And you hang the men."

The King watched the boy as his head nodded. Then he got up, lifted Daw from his stool, and put him into his own bed, where Daw fell asleep at once.

The King went out into the hall, where his friends were gathered round the fire. Sitting down with them, he said, "Is it true that the people are starving?"

"It was a poor harvest, and a hard winter," said one of his friends. "The poor always go hungry at such times."

"But not the rich?" the King said.

"The rich are wiser, and store food against hard times."

"The rich have money to buy food to store," said the King. "The poor do not. The rich can build safe, strong barns to store their food. The poor cannot."

His friend shrugged. "Maybe so. But that's the way things are. What can you do about it?"

7

Daw Comes Home

It was spring when Daw came home to his parents. Bright green leaves were on the trees, and green sprouts sprinkled the fields.

He came riding behind a huntsman of the King, on a horse with jingling bells on its harness. Before them and behind rode armed men in polished armour, and behind this troop of horsemen came carts, filled with barrels of flour and dried fish, parcels of raisins, jars of honey, joints of smoked meat, barrels of ale, and many other things. The food was a present from the King to Daw's parents, and the people of their village.

When the villagers saw the armed men coming, they were afraid, and hid.

They had seen nothing like it in their village before, and they thought these armed men were being sent to punish them for something – though they had no idea what they had done.

The King's men stopped in the middle of the village street. The carts drew up behind them. They waited, but no one appeared.

At last, the huntsman dismounted and

lifted Daw down from the horse's high back. He said, "Daw, lad, tell your people we're not going to hurt them. Tell them about the food."

Daw went down the street to his own house. He pushed open the door, and there were his mother and father, crouching by their fire, and staring at him in fear as he came in.

"Hello," he said. "I'm back."

They went on staring at him. They did not know him. The wolves had fed him, and the King had fed him, and he was a taller, plumper child than the one who'd been left in the forest. He was dressed in a fine suit of clothes too, that the King had given him, and his hair had been neatly cut. His parents thought he was a young prince, belonging to the party of rich people, with the armed men, who had just ridden into their village.

Daw said, "It's me. I've come home."

His mother squealed and hid her face. His father jumped to his feet and clenched his fists.

"We had nothing to feed you," he said. "We meant it for the best. Don't come as a ghost and haunt us now."

"I'm no ghost," Daw said, but when he moved towards them, they shrank back, fearing him.

He went outside and asked the carters to unload the food. He took a small barrel of wine, and a little packet of nuts and dried fruits, and carried it inside to his parents. Opening the food, he offered it to them, but they were almost too afraid to look at it. So Daw ate some of the fruit and nuts.

His mother watched him. Then she

said, "Ghosts don't eat and drink. They don't walk on the floor and open doors. This is Daw. He's alive." And then she hugged him and wept, while his father stood by, amazed.

"Where is your sister?" his mother

"Still with the wolves, if the King's men didn't kill her in the hunt." And Daw told them his long story.

"A miracle," said his mother. "A blessing. We may hope that Elka will come home."

Then she and Daw's father ran to find their neighbours, to tell them that they need not be afraid, and that the food in the carts was for them. The King's men all rode away, to find lodgings somewhere else, but all that day and until late into the night, the people of the village ran in and out of each other's houses, eating and drinking, and dancing and singing.

"Let's drink to the King's health!" someone said, and they cheered for the King who had given them this feast.

"If only," said the oldest woman in

the village, "the King had given us this food last year, when we needed it. There would have been more people to drink his health then."

Daw's mother held up her cup. "Let's drink to my daughter, Elka, and hope she comes home, like Daw!"

But years passed, and Elka didn't come home.

Daw grew from a boy to a young man. He was tall, and hard work made him strong, for he did more and more of the work on the farm. There were hungry times in those years, but they were never again so hungry as when he had been left in the forest. The harvests were better and, if they were poor, the King ordered his storehouses to be opened, and food was given to the people.

Often and often, as he was growing, Daw stood in the dark yard of his parents' house at night, and listened to the wolves howling in the mountains and forest. He knew their songs. He knew when they were calling the pack together for a hunt, and when they were singing to celebrate their catch.

When he listened to them, he remembered what it had been like to run as a wolf, and many a night he howled with them, calling to them. Sometimes he thought of searching the forest for a wolf's footprint that he could drink water from, and so turn into a wolf again. He thought of it often, but he didn't do it, having grown fond of his parents. They were old now, and he didn't want to leave them alone.

The other villagers, hearing him howling outside in the dark, laughed at him, and said he was mad. "There goes Wolf-Daw again," they said. "Howling at the moon."

One cold evening, when Daw stood in the yard, something moved in the grey moonlight. He started, peered – and saw a wolf slinking closer to him.

He held his breath.

The wolf nosed about in the moonlight, and then drank – from one of Daw's rain-filled footprints.

As soon as it had drunk, it rose upright, and unfolded into a girl. It was Elka.

Daw went to her, holding out his arms, but she stepped back.

"You smell of men," she said.

"You're safe!" he said. "I am so glad to

see you! Come in and see Mother and—"

"No," she said.

He thought that she didn't want to go into a house after spending so long in the forest. "I'll fetch them out here."

"No," she said.

He looked at her. She looked very strong, but thin, and fierce. He tried to go near to her again, but she moved sharply away from him.

"I'm glad the hunt didn't catch you," he said. "They caught me!" And he told her of how he'd been captured by the King's hunt, and all that had happened afterwards. He felt awkward as he told the story, for though she listened closely, she did not speak, and she paced from side to side in the little yard. "How did you get away?" he asked. "How have things been with you?"

"I was a wolf."

He waited for her to say more, but she said nothing. At every little sound from the houses nearby, she twitched and jumped.

"Never mind," Daw said. "You'll learn to chatter again, now you've come back to us."

"Come back?" she said, and laughed. "I am a wolf." As she turned away, she said, "The wolves have never turned me out." She crouched swiftly, drank from one of her own wolf-prints, and was a wolf again. As Daw shouted, she ran from the yard.

For the rest of the night, Daw stayed in the yard, calling and even howling like a wolf. The next night, and the next, and many, many nights after, for the rest of his life, he called. Even after he married, and had children of his own, he still called. He even ventured into the forests, howling to the wolves as he went.

"There goes mad Daw," said the villagers, when they heard him.

The wolf, that had been Elka, never came back.